Baxter and the
Golden Pavements

Baxter and the Golden Pavements

Anne Forsyth

Illustrated by Sally Holmes

HODDER AND STOUGHTON

LONDON   SYDNEY   AUCKLAND   TORONTO

Also by Anne Forsyth
Baxter the Travelling Cat

British Library Cataloguing in Publication Data

Forsyth, Anne
    Baxter and the golden pavements –
    (Hopscotch)
    I. Title
    823'.914[J]   PZ7
    ISBN 0-340-33854-7

First published 1984

Published by Hodder and Stoughton Children's Books,
a division of Hodder and Stoughton Ltd,
Mill Road, Dunton Green, Sevenoaks, Kent TN13 2YJ

Photoset by Rowland Phototypesetting Ltd,
Printed in Great Britain by St Edmundsbury Press,
Bury St Edmunds, Suffolk

Baxter was bored. He didn't like staying at home for long. He liked visiting.

Baxter was a large ginger cat with extra large paws. He visited lots of people. He called on

the old lady next door but one

the children at the school across the road

the newspaper shop on the corner.

Once, in a great adventure, he had even been to Scotland.

But now he had been at home for some time. And his giant ginger paws were itching to be off, travelling again.

Then one day he heard the children reading the story of Dick Whittington. He pricked up his ears and listened with interest to the story.

How Dick, a poor boy, set off to seek his fortune in London where, so people said, the streets were paved with gold.

How, with the help of his faithful cat, he became rich and was three times Lord Mayor of London.

Faithful cat!

City of London?

Pavements of gold!

Baxter made up his mind. 'That's where I'll go. I'll go to see the City of London,' he said to himself.

But how was he to get there? Baxter's home was on the outskirts of London, about thirty miles away. It was still a long journey to the City. So he sat and washed his paws and thought.

Then he remembered. Miss Smith! Miss Smith was an elegant Siamese cat who lived a few streets away.

She had a grand, very long name, but
Baxter just called her Miss Smith – very
politely. She didn't often speak to him,
except to boast about the cups and medals
she had won at cat shows. She thought he
was common.

Poor Miss Smith!

She didn't

    fight with other cats

    visit fish and chip shops

    or roam through the privet hedges.

She just sat around being beautiful. It
wouldn't have suited Baxter. But then,
no one had ever entered him for a
show.

Now Baxter remembered. Miss Smith
had told him she was to enter for another

cat show. It was to be this week, in London. Now was his chance.

He made sure he was looking at his best and went to call on her.

'Please,' he said, very humbly, 'when you go to London, can I come too?'

'Whatever for?' said Miss Smith scornfully. 'Don't say they're entering you for a show.'

Baxter bared his teeth. 'They wouldn't dare.'

He told her all about Dick Whittington, and the faithful cat, and how he was going to London to seek his fortune, just like Dick.

So she sniffed, rather grandly, and said, 'All right, then.'

Miss Smith travelled to shows in the back of a van, in her own special basket. When it was time to leave, Baxter climbed into the van and hid under an old rug. Miss Smith, looking even more beautiful than ever, was put into her basket, with her comb and her brush and everything she needed for the show, and they set off.

At last they reached London.

'I think we're here,' said Miss Smith, and Baxter peeped out from under the rug.

'I wish,' she said, 'that I was going with

you. But I have a very good chance of being champion this year.'

She closed one eye as she was carried away and Baxter raised a paw, as if he were saying, 'Good luck'.

Then he sniffed the air. He thought he could smell the river Thames. It was definitely London.

So he jumped out of the van and set off in the direction of the river.

He walked for a long time until he came to a large building with lots of turrets. Baxter was very curious. So he joined a long line of people filing in through the gateway.

'Well, just fancy!' he heard one of the visitors say. 'We really *are* at the Tower of London!'

The Tower of London!

Baxter was very excited. He'd heard all about the Tower and the famous Yeoman Warders – and there they were in their splendid uniforms, just like the pictures in a book.

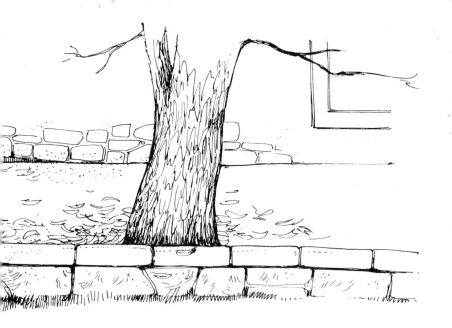

His whiskers twitched eagerly. Baxter followed the crowd through the gateways into the main part of the Tower. And he jumped on to a low wall so that he could see what was going on.

There, much to his surprise, were several large black birds. They were hopping about, paying no attention to anyone, just as if they owned the place.

'Don't you dare chase these ravens!' said a voice behind him.

Baxter turned round. There was a large glossy black cat looking sternly at him.

'Who are you?' asked the black cat.

'I'm Baxter. I'm . . . er . . . visiting,' said Baxter, rather timidly.

'I'm a Yeoman Warder Cat. In the service of the Queen. And these,' the black cat pointed a paw, 'are the Tower Ravens. If they ever fly away, the Tower will fall down. So we don't allow visiting cats too near them.'

'I didn't know,' said Baxter humbly.

Just fancy!

Suppose he *had* frightened the ravens!

And they'd flown away!

And the Tower had crumbled to the ground!

Baxter shivered at the thought.

'I'll show you round,' said the black cat in a more friendly tone.

It all seemed very strange to Baxter –

the towers with their winding staircases

and narrow passages

and cramped cells, where prisoners had been held long ago.

He found it rather dark and creepy. He didn't much care for the Tower with all the weapons and suits of armour. And he didn't like the stags' heads that looked down on him from the walls of the White Tower.

He almost expected them to speak. Still, he was a travelling cat and he had seen many strange things.

'Of course,' said the Yeoman Warder Cat as they walked across Tower Green, 'lots of people wouldn't care to spend a night here. I've even known cats that would be scared.'

'Not me,' said Baxter boldly. 'I wouldn't be scared of anything.

'I'm not scared of
    ghosts
    or savage beasts
    or anything creepy crawlie or spooky. Not me!'

Just then there was a wild, screeching noise.

'Whooooo . . . oooooh . . . Ha! Ha! Ha!'

Baxter ran as fast as his paws would carry him, down the path through the first gateway towards the entrance. He didn't stop till he was safely outside the walls of the Tower.

Behind him, the Yeoman Warder Cat looked up at a window. 'Dear me,' he

said. 'You shouldn't do that sort of thing.
You gave him quite a fright.'

'Ha! Ha! Ha!' screeched the parrot,
swinging on its perch at the window of
one of the Warders' houses. 'Pretty
polly – who's a pretty polly, then?'

'That was a narrow escape,' said Baxter
to himself. 'Well, I've seen the Tower.
Now I must find the golden pavements.'
So he set off again.

All through the City were great high buildings, streets thronged with people and traffic, and narrow little side alleys.

Baxter had never seen such tall buildings. He stopped to look at one very new block. It was so new that the workmen were just putting the finishing touches to the front entrance.

The building stretched up into the sky and it was all concrete and glass, as far as Baxter could see.

'Well, that's it,' said one of the workmen. 'Cement should soon be dry. That's a good job done.'

'Smashing,' said the other. 'Wouldn't mind being at the opening.' He laid down his trowel.

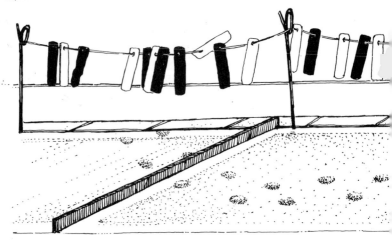

'Oh, well. Tea break now. Ready for a cuppa? Come on, let's go round to the café.'

Baxter was very curious. How did you get up there? Right to the sky? He decided to explore.

So he walked into the entrance – over the wet cement.

'Just a second,' called one workman to the other. 'Forgot my jacket.'

He turned back, stopped and glared. Then he shouted angrily at Baxter.

'Look! It's a cat! Gerrroff . . . you . . .'

Baxter realised he wasn't wanted here. It was better – and safer – to run as quickly as he could.

So he ran, leaving behind the angry shouts of the workmen and giant pawprints in the wet cement which said, just as plainly as if he had written his name: 'Baxter was here.'

By now, it was getting dark and the City was quiet. All the offices and shops were closed, and all the workers had gone home for the day. It was time for Baxter to move on. Besides, he was getting hungry. It was a long time since breakfast.

He trudged on until he came to an old

building with a splendid entrance.

Inside, he discovered a great hall with a decorated ceiling and many grand portraits on the walls. But there wasn't a crumb of food to be seen.

'I know! The kitchen! There is sure to be a kitchen in a place like this,' said Baxter, setting off for the basement.

And then he heard a sound from behind one of the doors.

'Miaouw . . . miaouw . . .'

He peeped inside.

Much to his surprise, there were at least a dozen cats. They were of different colours and sizes, but they all looked sleek and well-fed.

Sitting in the centre was a large tabby cat with a chain round his neck.

'A stranger! Who are you?' he said.

Baxter walked into the room. He wasn't afraid of anything. Besides, he was a very curious cat.

'My name is Baxter,' he said. 'I'm visiting.'

'In that case,' said the head cat graciously, 'you can join our meeting.'

'What kind of meeting is it?' asked Baxter. 'A mousers' club?'

'Mousers' club?' the head cat laughed scornfully. 'Oh, dear me, no. We are the Worshipful Company of Mousers. We look after the City. And we meet and dine here every week.'

'Except,' said a fat striped cat with white front and paws, 'that we haven't had our dinner yet.'

'Well, that's not my fault,' said the head cat, rather crossly.

He explained to Baxter. 'There was a banquet today. In the kitchen, behind that door, are all sorts of delicious left-overs – scraps of turkey, duck, lamb, roast beef, and salmon. Especially salmon. It's all there, behind the door.' He patted the door with his paw. 'If only we could get through the door.'

'But it isn't closed,' said Baxter. And sure enough, it wasn't. The door was slightly ajar. But the head cat kept patting it with his paw.

'You'll only close it, if you do that,' said Baxter. 'Look! This is how you do it.'

He hooked a great paw round the door and eased it open. It was a trick he had learned as a kitten – a trick he had often found useful.

All the Mousers became very excited.

'Good old Baxter! Well done, Baxter!' they cried, as they followed Baxter and the head cat into the kitchen.

There they found the turkey, duck, lamb and roast beef, and there lay the remains of the splendid salmon.

'Help yourself,' said the head cat.

All the cats ate with relish.

And they all agreed that Baxter should become a member of the Worshipful Company of Mousers.

Then most of them lay down to sleep in front of the kitchen stove.

'Won't you stay?' said the head cat next morning. 'There is a job in a city bank for a bright cat – good wages, all sorts of comforts.'

'No, thank you,' said Baxter. There was lots to see and he still hadn't found the golden pavements.

'Well,' said his new friend, 'there may be golden pavements, but I've never seen them. Try the Guildhall.'

So Baxter said goodbye to the City cats and moved on.

But still the pavements were made of stone, not gold, even when he reached the splendid Guildhall where the Lord Mayor and the Aldermen and Sheriffs meet.

He found his way into the Great Hall and looked up at the statues and the stained glass windows. Surely someone here could tell him where to find the golden pavements.

'Well, look at that!'

'Look at the size of those paws!'

'Large.'

'Very large, brother.'

'Giant-sized.'

Baxter couldn't think who was talking,
but they were quite clearly talking about
him. He looked all around the Great Hall
but he couldn't see anything. Then a voice
from above said, 'Cat!'

Baxter looked up and saw two great
wooden figures looking down at him.

They were very strange and really
rather ugly.

Both were wearing armour and
helmets. One held a spear. The other held
a long pole. At the end of the pole was a
spiked ball on a chain.

'Who are you?' he asked.

'We are giants,' said one of the figures.

'I am Gog,' said the one with the pole.

'And I am Magog,' said the one with the spear.

'We have been here for hundreds of
years,' said Gog.

'Off and on, brother.'

'Yes, off and on.'

'We stand here. We guard the City,'
said Magog.

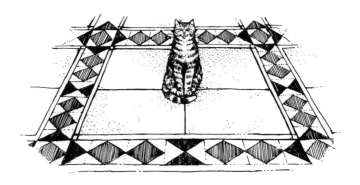

Baxter had never seen giants before, so he gazed in surprise.

'And who are you?' asked Gog in his deep voice.

'My name is Baxter and I am looking for the golden pavements.'

'Golden pavements!' said Gog. 'I don't remember seeing them.'

'Nor I,' said Magog.

They both thought for a bit.

'You have very large paws,' said Magog.

'Extra large,' said Gog.

'I have,' said Baxter modestly, 'been mistaken for a lion – from time to time, by people who saw my paws under a door. Only the paws, you understand.'

'All the same,' said Gog, 'a giant among cats.'

'Do you think, brother . . .?' said Magog.

'Why not?'

'Let's ask him.'

Gog said, 'My brother and I have been looking at you. You are clearly a sensible cat, as well as having giant paws. So you would be very suited to help us guard the City. You see,' he went on, 'my brother stands at one end of the gallery. I stand at the other. You could stand – or
sit – between us. It would be pleasant company for us.'

'One day,' said Magog, 'they might put you on a coat of arms.'

(A coat of arms is a special kind of badge that belongs to a family or a city, like the City of London.)

'Thank you,' said Baxter. 'It is a great honour. But I don't belong here. I have only come to the City to find the golden pavements. I am a cat that likes travelling.

So I must move on.'

'A great pity,' said Gog.

'Yes, indeed,' said Magog.

They waved the pole and the spear to
Baxter as they said goodbye, and he
waved a paw to them in return.

By the end of that day Baxter felt rather
tired. He still hadn't found the golden
pavements, and the stony streets were
very hard on the paws.

So he began to look for somewhere to
sleep.

Suddenly he came to a little yard, and
there was a lorry. On top of the lorry was
a little house. Baxter had seen plenty of
lorries and he had seen plenty of houses,
but he had never seen a house on top of a
lorry.

It had

a roof thatched with straw

windows and door

and a little garden with grass and tubs
of flowers.

Baxter was rather puzzled. Was he dreaming? What was a house doing on top of a lorry?

And what a strange sort of house! There was nothing inside.

No beds
No tables
No chairs.

But he was very tired. So he decided he would go to sleep, and find out in the morning just where he was.

So he went into the little house and lay down in a corner and curled up in a ball. Before long he was sound asleep.

It was daylight when he awoke. He could hear voices.

'Oh, my costume's too tight!'

'Is my hat all right?'

'Here, you must have a flag to wave!'

'I wish I'd eaten more breakfast – I'm hungry!'

'Isn't it exciting!'

Baxter peered out. There, round the little house, were about half-a-dozen children, all dressed up in old-fashioned clothes.

Some of the boys wore short jackets and breeches and had little caps on their heads.

The girls wore flowery dresses with full skirts and bonnets with ribbons.

'Look what I've found!'

One of the windows opened and Baxter found himself looking at a small boy, dressed in an old-fashioned costume just like the rest.

'Look, it's a cat!'

'A ginger cat!'

'What's it doing here?'

'Look at its huge paws!'

Baxter was very surprised. What was happening?

Then along came the woman who was in charge.

'A city cat!' she said, bending down to look through the window. 'Just like Dick Whittington's cat. That should bring us luck! We must take him to the police station,' she went on. 'But we haven't time just now.'

'Let him come with us,' shouted the children. 'He can be in the procession.'

'All right,' said the woman. 'We'll take him to the police station when it's all over.'

Baxter stretched himself and made his way out of the house. He looked around. There were all sorts of odd figures walking about.

There was

a huge milk bottle
a slice of bread on legs
a walking pillar box
a panda
an emu
and a life-sized cow.

And what was even stranger – all these
figures were talking to one another.
Baxter couldn't believe his eyes.

'Roll up! Roll up!' called a clown,
walking, a little unsteadily, on stilts. 'Roll
up for the Lord Mayor's Show!'

The Lord Mayor's Show! So that was
it! That was why everyone was dressed
up. And the little house wasn't a real
house. It was to be one of the floats in the
procession.

And he, Baxter, was going to be part of
the Lord Mayor's Show.

Soon, the bands started up and the first floats set off. In the distance, Baxter could hear cheering and see flags waving.

When Baxter's float started to move along the street, he took up a place in the little garden. The children leant out of the window and threw sweets to the crowd, and everyone shouted and waved their flags.

'Hurray!'

'Look, it's a real cat!'

So Baxter got a special cheer all to himself.

Baxter's family – the Carrs – had set off from home by train in good time. As soon as they arrived in the City, they found a place on the edge of the pavement, where they would have a fine view.

The children were very excited.

'Will the Lord Mayor be wearing his robes?'

'Is it really a golden coach?'

'Just like Dick Whittington?'

They could hardly wait for the procession to begin.

First came the City Police and the Police band, then sailors and soldiers and more bands. The children liked the splendid Shire horses from the City breweries, and gave them a special cheer. And then there were all the floats from the stores and the banks and every so often another band. They laughed at the milk bottles and the slices of bread and the pillar box on legs, and all the people dressed up as animals.

And then . . .
'Oh, look at the little house!'
'There's a cat in the garden!'
'It's rather like Baxter!'
'It's *very* like Baxter!'
'It *is* Baxter!'
'Baxter! Baxter!'

Baxter was very pleased that so many people seemed to be calling his name and he sat very proudly among the flags and balloons and cheers. And he didn't even notice his own family, jumping up and down, and calling to him.

'Don't worry,' said the children's mother. 'When it's all over, we'll go and find him.'

'Baxter was the best bit of the whole

show,' said the children.

But there was even more to come. The cheering got louder and there were the Aldermen and Sheriffs, leaning out of carriages and vintage cars and waving. And then – the Lord Mayor himself, in his splendid robes and gold chain – in the golden coach, drawn by six grey horses and guarded by the City pikemen.

When it was all over and the City dustcarts were sweeping up the rubbish, the Carr family went up to a policeman and explained how they'd seen Baxter, their lost cat. He told them how to get to the place where the floats were parked.

People were pushing and jostling and it took a long time. But at last they reached the yard. There was the little house. And there were the children, drinking lemonade and feeding Baxter on sardine sandwiches.

The Carrs explained about Baxter. About how he liked travelling and how no other cat in England – no, Britain! – had paws as large as his.

And the woman in charge said, 'Fancy! He really is a remarkable cat!'

Baxter was surprised to see his family. And he was very pleased when he heard that they were all going home. Because the streets of London were very hard –

and they weren't paved with gold after all. And he hadn't made his fortune. But what a lot of adventures he had had!

When they got home, he ate up every scrap of dinner. Then he washed his face and paws and settled down to sleep. It was good to be home again!

Next day he called on Miss Smith.

'Oh,' she said, rather coldly, '*you're* back. This time,' she went on, without waiting for him to speak, 'I won a medal and a year's supply of cat food.'

'Oh?' said Baxter. 'I went to the Tower and saw the ravens and a Yeoman Warder Cat. And I joined the Worshipful Company of Mousers and dined on salmon. And I met two giants. But best of all,' he said, 'I was part of the Lord Mayor's Show.'

'Some cats,' said Miss Smith, turning her back on him, 'have all the luck.'